UNDYING TALES

MYTHOLOGIES OF SPECIES ON THE VERGE OF EXTINCTION

BY STEPHANIE LAW

www.eyeofnewtpress.com

TABLE OF CONTENTS

CREATOR INTRODUCTION 6
SPECIALIST INTRODUCTION 8
ALCATHOE BAT | PÚCA 11
ANDEAN BEAR | UKUKUS 12
AXOLOTL | XOLOTYL 15
AZUERO SPIDER MONKEY | WOODEN PEOPLE 16
BENGAL TIGER | BONBIBI 19
BLUE-THROATED HILLSTAR | VIRACOCHA 20
BLUE WHALE | CETUS 23
BOG TURTLE | SKY WOMAN 24
BOREAL WOODLAND CARIBOU | KANIPINIKASSIKUEU 27
BROWN EARED-PHEASANT | FENGHUANG 28
BUMBLEBEE | MELISSAE 31
CANADA WARBLER | ENDLESS WINTER 32
DARWIN'S FOX | GURUVILU 35
DUSKY GOPHER FOX | THE GREAT FROG 36
EASTERN SPOTTED SKUNK | SKUNK ORIGIN TALE 39
EUROPEAN OAK | TREE OF LIFE 40
FINNISH FOREST REINDEER | HUNTER CONSTELLATION 43
FOUR-BLOTCHED UMBRELLA OCTOPUS | TUHI-RANGI/PELORUS JACK 44
GOLDEN-CAPPED FRUIT BAT | ASWANG 47
GOLDEN SNUB-NOSED MONKEY | SUN WUKONG 48
HAINAN MAGPIE | THE COWHERD AND THE WEAVERGIRL 51
HISPID HARE | THE RABBIT IN THE MOON 52
KIRIKUCHI CHAR | FUNAYŪREI 55
LONG-SNOUTED SEAHORSE | HIPPOCAMPUS 56
LONG-WHISKERED OWLET | OWL SPIRIT ANIMAL LORE 59

Undying Tales

by Stephanie Law

For Claire Miranda Dawes,
that your world may always
contain such wonders.

Undying Tales
Mythologies of species on the verge of extinction

Published by Eye of Newt Books Inc. • www.eyeofnewtpress.com
Eye of Newt Books Inc. 614 Mount Pleasant Road, Unit 2, Toronto, Ontario, M4S 2M8

Library and Archives Canada Cataloguing in Publication

Title: Undying tales / by Stephanie Law.
Names: Law, Stephanie Pui-Mun, author, illustrator.
Description: Includes bibliographical references.
Identifiers: Canadiana 20230621627 | ISBN 9781738124602 (hardcover)
Subjects: LCSH: Endangered species—Mythology. | LCSH: Endangered species—Folklore.
Classification: LCC GR705 .L39 2024 | DDC 398/.369—dc23

ISBN: 978-1-7381246-0-2

10 9 8 7 6 5 4 3 2 1

Printed in China

LUSCHAN'S SALAMANDER | DRAGON 60
MALLEE EMU-WREN | OOZLUM BIRD 63
MARGAY CAT | DOMINGO'S CAT 64
MIGRATORY MONARCH | DAUGHTER OF THE SUN/ITZPAPALOTL 67
MOJAVE DESERT TORTOISE | MASTAMBO 68
ORNATE EAGLE RAY | GUARDIAN SPIRITS/KAITIAKI 71
PACIFIC POCKET MOUSE | STEALING OF FIRE 72
PHILIPPINE EAGLE-OWL | DALIKMATA 75
RED WOLF | PAWNEE NATION/WOLF STAR 76
RESPLENDENT QUETZAL | QUETZALCOATL 79
RIVERINE RABBIT | THE ORIGIN OF DEATH 80
ROWAN | PREN CERDINEN 83
SCOTTISH WILDCAT | CAIT SIDHE 84
SEA OTTER | KUSHTAKA 87
SEYCHELLES WOLF SNAKE | MAMI WATA 88
SLENDER-SNOUTED CROCODILE | CROCODILE ORIGIN TALE 91
SUN BEAR | ONG TROI 92
TEMMINCK'S PANGOLIN | PANGOLIN ORIGIN TALE 95
TIBETAN ANTELOPE | THE GOLDEN FLEECE 96
TRI-SPINE HORSESHOE CRAB | KABUTOGANI 99
UMBRELLA THORN ACACIA | THE TREE OF LIFE AND DEATH 100
VIRGINIA BIG-EARED BAT | DJOGEON/GANDAYAH 103
WHALE SHARK | WHALE SHARK ORIGIN TALE 104
WHITE-NAPED CRANE | CHINESE CRANE LORE 107
YANGTZE GIANT SOFTSHELL TURTLE | LAKE OF THE RETURNED SWORD 108
WORKS REFERENCED 110
ABOUT THE AUTHOR 113

CREATOR INTRODUCTION

Humans have told stories about human existence on planet Earth since before written record — these are our oral traditions, myths, and legends. These tales often tackle the beginnings of human life on Earth, and they often start with phrases like: *When the world was young*...; *In the beginning*...; *First there was only darkness*...; *Long ago*...; *Before the world existed*...etc. These are the words that launch a primal narrative. Every culture tells such tales to describe the earliest beginnings of the world, to explain how all the wonders that we live with and see today came to be, and how humans have coped within this world. All peoples look around themselves, at the earth and sky, at the mountains, rivers, forests, and seas, at the unimaginable variety of living creatures that populate those vast reaches, and they wonder, and they marvel, and then they craft and tell tales.

The natural world is a fountain of inspiration for storytellers and artists, me included. The Undying Tales project began in 2019 as a daily drawing challenge. The challenge became a favourite of mine and my online community and quickly became an annual event during which I invited other artists to join me on a month-long journey delving into tales from around the world and highlighting species from the IUCN's Red List. The project explores the relationship between human understanding and storytelling and the natural world. Nature can be a terrible destructive force, but it is also humanity's sustenance and home. Humans are intimately tied into a vast web of life, and our actions have reverberations throughout that web, for good or for ill. The difference being we have a will to change our actions.

As an artist, I feel the organic pulse of life and growth and decay in the rhythms of my compositions. I trace the shapes of tree branches in my abstractions. I dive into the human collective subconscious of mythic associations with animals.

I see the source of my inspiration fading around me.

I see calls to action: some of them are successful, some are not. I see environmental despair, and I see actionable hope. I see that we collectively must make individual changes, and I also see that we are small pieces within a larger and slow-moving framework that must be pushed socially and politically into change.

I don't want to see a day when the resplendent quetzal is only remembered by the mythos of the Ancient Aztec deity, Quetzalcoatl, and the ethereally shimmering, metallic blue-green relics made from the quetzal's feathers; or when the sun bear is relegated to the heavens as an embodiment of light rather than roaming through forests and swamps. I want the ocean to continue to be filled with the leviathan shadows of blue whales, whale sharks, and ornate eagle rays so when they breach the surface of the waves and we catch fleeting glimpses of their majesty, we feel a link to them and to our ancestors who stood upon the rocking decks of ships, or upon shorelines, and told tales of these wonders they spied. And I want to know they will continue to inspire tales when the wind has scattered my sandy footprints and the water's surface is mirror-flat again.

I want to interact with a living world, even as I soak in the experiences of that world and distill it into lines and brushstrokes of pigment on paper. I am a storyteller whose words are images, and I tread along paths that others have forged before me. I know the beginning of these tales, and I do not want to see them come to an end.

Stephanie Law
Artist

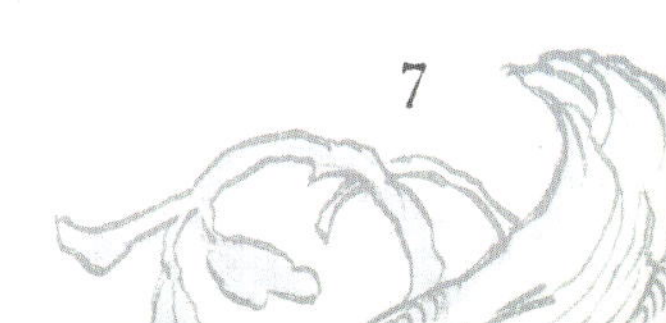

SPECIALIST INTRODUCTION

Our planet and its inhabitants are in trouble. The evidence of this is all around us, from the growing number and intensity of adverse weather events to the increasing unpredictability of the seasons and the disappearance of plants and animals that we once took for granted. Anthropogenic climate change is only one of the causes of biodiversity loss: the variety and richness of life on Earth are also threatened directly by overexploitation, habitat destruction, and other negative consequences of the prioritization of economic growth over our shared wellbeing. Indeed, the deleterious impacts of human activities are so obvious that scientists recognize that we are now living in a geological epoch defined by them, the Anthropocene.

Impacts on flora and fauna can be measured in different ways. The regularly updated IUCN Red List of Threatened Species uses a mix of indicators to assess relative risk, assigning each species to one of eight categories: Extinct, Extinct in the Wild, Critically Endangered, Endangered, Vulnerable, Near Threatened, Least Concern, or Data Deficient. These and other data can be analyzed to produce global estimates. One study published in 2023, for example, found that 48% of sampled animal populations were declining, but only 3% increasing; another estimated that 45% of flowering plant species were at risk of extinction.

These are alarming figures that corroborate the conclusion that we are living through an extinction crisis of our own making, and that will perhaps be our own end. As its begetters, we also have the power to change our behavior and reduce the harm that we are inflicting on the species that we still share this fragile planet with. It is widely acknowledged that to preserve biodiversity and all its benefits we need to take collective action at every level of society, from the local to the global. This includes protecting and restoring natural habitats and ecosystems, as well as reducing different forms of overexploitation and the unsustainable use of natural resources.

We already know a lot about how to begin doing this and how we might contribute to conservation as individuals, as a quick search of the web will illustrate (try phrases such as "How can biodiversity be preserved?" and "How can I help conservation?"). However, as successive UN climate change conferences have shown, we struggle when change is resisted by powerful vested interests. How do we transform "business as usual" and the global political economy that has enabled the current crisis? There is no simple answer to this question, but part of the solution is surely by changing minds, by raising public awareness about biodiversity loss and conservation, and by educating present and future decision-makers, whoever and wherever they may be.

This is where *Undying Tales* comes into its own. In recent years there has been an efflorescence of creative work around the extinction crisis as visual artists, poets, musicians, and many others around the world have responded imaginatively to it. With its magical illustrations and well-crafted vignettes of endangered species and the mythologies woven around them in different cultures, Stephanie Law's book makes an original contribution to this burgeoning tradition. It is marvelous in every sense, and each double spread is not only wonderful to behold, but also informative, fascinating, thought-provoking.

It is often said, paraphrasing Claude Lévi Strauss, that animals are "good to think with," an observation that is readily extended to plants and other forms of life when anthropologists seek to explain the role played by the natural world in myth and folktales. *Undying Tales* reminds us how apt this phrase is and how closely intertwined people's explanations of the world are with the animate life they share it with. Our knowledge of such narratives and the practices associated with them is as patchy as that of our understanding of the biology of many natural species, including their potential medicinal and other uses. And yet they can play a vital role in both informing and motivating conservation education and action, just as this book does.

When species disappear from the tangled web of life, our planet is diminished accordingly. When we lose them from our lives, we lose all the benefits that they can provide, including those that are unrealized. We also lose the local knowledge and stories that are told about them unless they have been carefully recorded. Whatever you can do to support conservation, also consider the possible value of such narratives and how they might help, if only through retelling and depicting them as they are in *Undying Tales*. If you get a chance to collect such stories yourself, then please do, and give a thought to how they might be disseminated and used to ensure that the species they are about both escape extinction and continue to thrive.

Martin Walsh

Dr. Martin Walsh
Cambridge University
Social Anthropology Department

ALCATHOE BAT

Myotis alcathoe | DATA DEFICIENT

There is a mischievous, shape-changing sprite called the Púca (poo-ka) in Ireland where the bat is native. Púca can take on the shape of various creatures, even human form, though it can give itself away by some lingering animal attribute like long furred ears, or a tail beneath clothing. One of the shapes it is said to take on is that of a bat, to flit through the night on silent leathery wings and slip through the tangled branches of forests. The Púca is often described as capricious in its dealings with humans, at times benevolent and at other times malicious. In Irish folklore the Púca waits along roadsides for unsuspecting humans that it can play with. If you come across a Púca, be sure to treat it with respect or else earn its ire!

It has been speculated that the character of Puck, Robin Goodfellow, in Shakespeare's *A Midsummer Night's Dream* was inspired by this creature. "Lord, what fools these mortals be!" is one of Puck's most famous lines from the play. The name "Alcathoe" is taken from the Ancient Greek myth where Minyas' daughter, Alcathoe, spurned Dionysus who responded by turning her into a bat.

The Alcathoe bat is a mysterious and rare species, and so there is not enough data to place it on the endangered species list; however, it is considered threatened. Bats are pollinators and they suffer for many of the same reasons other pollinators do — loss of breeding ground and habitat. As native vegetation is replaced by grassy lawns, non-native crops and gardens, and roads, all pollinators are losing the space they need to survive.

Pronunciation: Al-cat-ho-e

ANDEAN BEAR

TREMARCTOS ORNATUS | VULNERABLE

In Peru, there are stories of the Ukukus. They are trickster bear beings who are born of a bear father and a human mother. They possess supernatural strength, and though mostly well intentioned, their unexpected power can catch even themselves by surprise and wreak havoc.

Each year, the Qoyllur Rit'i festival is a celebration of the stars as the Pleiades constellation comes into view in the night sky. Dancers, musicians, and a procession of indigenous people from the region climb high into the mountains to be touched by the first rays of the Winter Solstice sun.

Climbing even higher, the Ukukus, celebrants who take on the role of the trickster bears, proceed up to the glaciers and return with blocks of ice to be melted and used for medicinal and healing ceremonies. Sadly, with the receding glaciers, this final portion of the festival is no longer performed, and the diminishing ice is left in the unreachable glacial heights.

The Andean bear, also known as the spectacled bear, inhabits the cloud forests of the Andes mountains. This habitat has become fragmented from human development and destruction. Habitat loss forces the bears into more frequent contact with humans, which exposes these creatures to hunting.

AXOLOTL

Ambystoma mexicanum | CRITICALLY ENDANGERED

To the Aztecs, axolotl was a creature linked with death and transformation. It was the animal form of the Aztec god, Xolotl. Xolotl had a twin brother named Quetzalcoatl. The brothers embarked on a journey to the underworld in order to retrieve some bone relics from the goddess Mictlantecuhtli, whom they had to trick in order to win the bones. They fled back above to the light of the living world with their prize. With the help of the gods, from these ancient bones, humans were born.

In another story, Xolotl fled from death. He disguised himself repeatedly, first as a corn plant, then a maguey plant, and was uncovered each time. Finally, he took on the form of a salamander (an axolotl, as it came to be called, stemming from Xolotl's name), and fled into the water, but death found him regardless.

Axolotls are one of the remaining links that contemporary Mexicans have with their Aztec ancestors and are now critically endangered for a number of reasons. Pollution and habitat loss play a large part in this species' reduced numbers. In addition, invasive species have had a detrimental effect on both the axolotls and their habitat. Creatures such as perch and pickerel were introduced to the axolotl's habitat altering it and consuming many axolotl.

Pronunciation: Ak-suh-laa-tl

AZUERO SPIDER MONKEY

ATELES GEOFFROYI AZUERENSIS
CRITICALLY ENDANGERED

In the creation myth of the Maya, the gods went through several iterations in their attempts to make mankind. In one of these earlier cycles of creation, humans were made of wood. These people of wood were foolish. They were wasteful and ungrateful to the gods, and so the gods decided to destroy the wooden men. In some stories it is a great flood that brings about the end, in other tales jaguars do the work for the gods, and from time to time, it is statues come to life that destroy the wooden men.

A few of the wooden men managed to escape the retribution, however, and those were transformed into monkeys, to live on today as ancestors of mankind from a previous cycle of the gods' creation. Man, as we move through the world today, was crafted by the gods from maize.

Tropical dry forest once covered the Azuero peninsula — not so today. Forest remnants large enough to support the Azuero spider monkey populations are rare, which also makes them easily found. Hunting and deforestation are the greatest threats to this unique creature.

Pronunciation: Ah-zoo-row

BENGAL TIGER

PANTHERA TIGRIS TIGRIS | ENDANGERED

The Sundarbans is a region of coastal mangrove swamps in a delta formed by the Padma, Brahmaputra, and Meghna Rivers in the Bay of Bengal. In the tangled forests of mangroves, sand dunes, and mudflats, live tigers. They are not only feared for their deadliness, but also revered for being protectors and incarnations of the gods and goddesses within the bounds of the Sundarbans.

The goddess Bonbibi is the incarnation of the forest itself, and those who venture into the swamps seek her blessing for protection. Bonbibi is often depicted riding atop a tiger. The tiger is a god who punishes those who deplete the wealth of the domain without heeding the rules that govern sustainable harvesting of natural resources.

Tigers are emblematic of the tension between humans and the land: while humans live off the land, reaping its gifts and rewards, they must as a result be at the mercy of the vagaries and sometimes implacable reality of nature. Bengal tigers are threatened by poachers and habitat loss. There are very few individuals living in the wild, and the available habitat now is not large enough to support any population growth.

BLUE-THROATED HILLSTAR

Oreotrochilus cyanolaemus
CRITICALLY ENDANGERED

Flitting at high altitudes among the flowers in the remote ranges of the Andes mountains of Ecuador, the blue-throated hillstar is a flash of deep blue and green across the landscape.

In a pre-Incan legend in Peru, the condor was once king of the skies and messenger to the heavens. It was he who communicated the supplications and prayers to the creator, Viracocha. The condor would take the messages from humans and convey them, but even given this celestial charge, he had never laid eyes upon Viracocha's visage, for he was not permitted to do so.

The hummingbird was a much more unassuming creature than the grand condor, but she had a knowledge of the world gleaned from sipping at the nectar that was the essence of the flowers and plants. She was also a curious and creative creature.

One day the hummingbird stowed away in the condor's feathers as the condor flew with messages to Viracocha. When they came into the heavenly sphere, the hummingbird emerged and looked and basked in the radiance of the divine visage, and was transformed and elevated in that moment. Thereafter, the condor conceded that while he would be the king and protector of the skies, the hummingbird would take on the mantle of messenger and spiritual guide.

The blue-throated hillstar is critically endangered. There is only one very small population of them in the Andes mountains, and as such, a single threatening event can rapidly affect all these creatures at once, putting them at great risk for extinction.

BLUE WHALE

Balaenoptera musculus | ENDANGERED

In Ancient Greek myths, cetea were leviathan sea creatures. The Ancient Greeks imagined them as sea monsters, but they were most likely inspired by whales.

Queen Cassiopeia of Aethiopia was a vain woman, not only of herself; but she was also overly proud of her daughter Andromeda's beauty. She boasted that Andromeda was more lovely than the Nereids (sea nymphs). This angered Poseidon, god of the sea, who sent a cetus (or sea monster) to attack the city of the boastful queen.

The king and queen belatedly became fearful. They consulted an oracle, who told them they must sacrifice their daughter Andromeda to appease Poseidon. In great distress, but with no other alternative for salvation, they chained Andromeda to a rock by the sea as an offering to the cetus and Poseidon. The hero Perseus freed her and slew the cetus, leaving Queen Cassiopeia to pay the price for her vanity.

Commercial whaling in earlier centuries greatly reduced the blue whales' global numbers, and current primary threats are environmental changes, vessel strikes, and ocean noise. Because whales are so enormous and long-lived, they accumulate a significant amount of carbon in their bodies during their lifetime. Blue whales help to regulate krill populations, which are tied to the health of phytoplankton and algae on which they feed.

BOG TURTLE

Glyptemys muhlenbergii
CRITICALLY ENDANGERED

Many of the indigenous peoples of the Northeastern Woodlands share a tale of how the world began, and of a turtle who carries the world upon his back. In ancient times, there was a world above the dome of the sky. In this upper world, the Great Chief and other beings knew nothing of what lay below their domed crust. In the center of their world grew an enormous tree laden with sweet flowers and fruit.

The Great Chief found cause to have the tree uprooted, and in so doing revealed a yawning pit. Sky Woman was drawn to it by her curiosity, and the Great Chief pushed her through. As she tumbled through the vast space between, she was aided by waterfowl who softened her fall, and at last she landed upon the back of a turtle of the underworld. All about was watery darkness and no land.

Animals from this world attempted to swim down under the waves to help Sky Woman. Otter, muskrat, beaver, and toad all tried, and though the stories vary, one or another of these creatures at last succeeded and brought up mud. From this earthly mud, and from the sky dirt and seeds from the celestial tree that Sky Woman had in her hands during her fall, it is said that solid earth formed, and the world below sprang to life.

Bog turtles are extremely sensitive to the effects of global warming. Erratic weather patterns are disrupting the fragile balance key to the turtle's survival. By altering hydrological cycles, global warming will either dry out or flood the turtle's habitat. As the changing climate alters the availability of the turtle's current habitat, they will have very limited ability to migrate to places that could sustain them.

BOREAL WOODLAND CARIBOU

Rangifer tarandis caribou
ENDANGERED

Caribou have an essential relationship with the Innu Tribes, for the nomadic tribes relied on meat and hides from these animals while also deeply respecting the spirit of the creatures. For the Innu, the spirit world is bound to the real world seamlessly, and the shamans would communicate with the spirits with their drums. Animal Masters within Innu mythology are supernatural beings who give the people permission to hunt the creatures in a respectful way, for food and for the materials to support their livelihood. They ensure that the people follow the traditions and hunting rituals, or else face famine and repercussions.

Among the Animal Masters, Caribou Man (Kanipinikassikueu) is one of the most important leaders. He is sometimes said to have once been a man who fell in love with a caribou-woman and was transformed into a caribou. This marriage and transformation between human and caribou highlight the mutual nature of the relationship of hunter and animal, and how life is thus granted by sacrifice.

The primary danger to boreal woodland caribou is human-caused change to habitat through development, fragmentation, and degradation, as well as industrial-scale resource extraction. Survival of roaming woodland caribou depends on maintaining large, unbroken swaths of the forest for their migration, as these animals avoid human and predator interaction by following selected forested routes.

BROWN EARED-PHEASANT

CROSSOPTILON MANTCHURICUM
VULNERABLE

The Chinese Fenghuang, the king of the birds, is a mythical creature that only appears in peaceful and prosperous states. It is often called a phoenix, but it is a very different creature from the Ancient Greek mythological concept of a "phoenix" (a singular creature that dies in flame and is reborn). In the Tang dynasty (618–906), a common decorative motif was of a Fenghuang circling peonies. The delicate feathered tail weaves playfully among the blooms. It was a symbol of harmony and prosperity, often used as the insignia of princesses.

The Fenghuang is a beautiful and immortal being that has a pheasant's head and body, peacock's tail, crane's legs, and swallow's wings. Sightings of it were seen as an omen of political harmony and world peace upon an Emperor's ascension. The Fenghuang encapsulates both female and male energies within itself, thus being a physical embodiment of tranquility, harmony, and of yin and yang in balance.

The brown eared-pheasant, with its beautiful tail, is a species that largely lives in protected areas; however, elsewhere this species is poached for its tail feathers and is suffering from habitat loss due to deforestation, climate change, and human development.

BUMBLEBEE

Bombus subterraneus | LEAST CONCERN

Bees have had a presence in human mythologies from around the world for centuries. In 3500 B.C., Upper and Lower Egypt were ruled by kings whose respective hieroglyphics were of a reed and a bee, and Egypt was described in the Bible as a land "flowing with milk and honey."

The name "Melissa" has its origins in Ancient Greece, where the priestesses of Demeter, Artemis, and Persephone were called Melissae, meaning bees, and some of them were gifted with the art of foretelling. The art of beekeeping was venerated, and throughout the Middle Ages bees were associated with the gods, magic, prophecy, and fairies.

The sixteenth century Italian poet Ludovico Ariosto wrote an epic poem *Orlando Furioso* ("The Madness of Orlando"). The tale tells of a world inhabited by fantastic creatures, monsters, and sorcerers against a backdrop of war and chivalric romance. In the poem, there is a good sorceress named Melissa, who is an acolyte of Merlin and has the gift of foresight, which she uses to ensure the union of two lovers.

Globally, bee populations have been suffering due to climate change, pesticide use, and destruction of native habitat and flora. People often hear of the plight of honeybees, but those are not endangered. The native wild populations of bees are the ones at risk. These wild native bees are vital to our agriculture as crop pollinators, and they are supplemented but not replaced by cultivated honeybees. The best way to help bees is to focus on local habitats so that native bees might remain.

CANADA WARBLER

Cardellina canadensis
LEAST CONCERN

There is an Ojibwe legend of an endless winter. There was a man who captured all the summer birds: warblers, doves, finches, woodpeckers, and sparrows. The year cycled around, and the time came for the sun to warm the frozen ground, and for green things to grow, and the air to fill with the wings of birds and insects, but all was still and cold in the land. Winter held sway through the spring and summer because the birds were held captive.

As the people and animals shivered, food grew sparse. They held council and it was decided that the Fisher would set forth to find what was causing the unending winter, and to bring the summer birds back. After a long journey, the Fisher arrived at the man's stronghold and found it guarded by crows. He sealed the crows' beaks shut with a bit of wax, the only item he had taken with him on his journey, so they could cry no warning to their master. When he found all the cages, he tore them open with his teeth. The birds lifted their wings and one by one soared away. In their wake, the air warmed, the land thawed, and spring and summer returned in a rush to bathe the land in growth and awakening.

The Canada Warbler spends most of its time in Canada but winters in the Andes, where deforestation for lumber and farmland means large-scale habitat loss for the Warbler. This species was listed as threatened in 2008 by the Committee on the Status of Endangered Wildlife in Canada, and in 2010 after protective actions it was relisted as special concern.

DARWIN'S FOX

Lycalopex fulvipes | ENDANGERED

Legends of the Guruvilu "fox snake" can be found among the Mapuche people of Chile. The first published record of this mythical creature was in the observations of a Jesuit priest by the name of Felipe Gómez de Vidaurre, in the late eighteenth century. His sources told him this beast had the head of a vixen and the serpentine body of a snake. Several accounts in the decades that followed — from successive missionaries, exploration expeditions, and military campaigns in the region — mentioned a fox-snake-dragon-cat-like creature that lived in the ponds, rivers, and lakes, enticing passersby to their death in deceptively calm waterways. It moved with surprising speed and strength and was agile in the water.

Some folklorists think otters might be the original inspiration for the stories of Guruvilu and might explain the claims of sightings, though it is always described as fox-headed.

The Darwin's fox is named for the explorer because he discovered this rare species and noted its difference from the other native canines. It resides on a small island in South America and on the Chilean mainland. The main threat to these creatures is fragmentation of their native habitat. They are also facing threats from injury and disease spread through feral dogs.

DUSKY GOPHER FROG

LITHOBATES SEVOSUS
CRITICALLY ENDANGERED

Frogs are ubiquitous amphibians, swimming through freshwater streams, ponds, marshes, and wetlands. They are the sentinels of waterways — if they are silenced it is a portent that greater ills are coming. Frogs cast a long shadow in the imaginations of many cultures. Sometimes they are associated with the bringing of rain, sometimes with the cessation of rain. Sometimes they are worshipped as the emissaries of the gods or feared as witches' familiars. They sing from the reeds and mud banks in a hypnotic rhythm that is like a chant of power.

In Cherokee lore, solar and lunar eclipses happen when the great frog in the sky is trying to swallow the sun or moon. The tribe would come together and beat their drums to frighten off the great frog so that the celestial light could once again emerge.

The gopher frog's range is very small and specific, and so they are highly vulnerable to changes in their habitat, which has become fragmented by human development, particularly roads and fire suppression. Gopher frogs thrive in forests that burn naturally and regularly. When humans intervene to suppress or stop forest fires altogether it alters the ecosystem and negatively affects species that rely on the regular burn cycle to thrive.

EASTERN SPOTTED SKUNK

Spilogale putorius | VULNERABLE

The Winnebago Tribe tells a story of the origin of skunks: There was once a young girl who was exquisitely beautiful. She had long hair that was pure white, and of which she was extremely vain. Many suitors came to call upon her and seek her favour, but she disdained them all, preferring instead to admire her own reflection in the water, and to rub sweet-smelling flowers into her skin to perfume her body.

One day, yet another young man came to her, and she immediately turned her nose up at him. She laughed and mocked his unbecoming looks and his wrinkled, ugly skin. Unfortunately for her, it was no ordinary man, but Turtle in human guise. The spirit shed the human form and stood before her as Turtle. He declared that she had rejected one of the great spirits, all while thinking herself holy because of her beautiful appearance. As punishment, she would now be what she had mocked.

As he spoke, she shrank into a small, furry body, covered with black hair but for white streaks, the only trace of her once-glorius hair. The scent of flowers faded from her and was replaced by an odious scent that caused all those nearby to flee at her approach.

The decline of this species' population, so marked that it has been listed as vulnerable, is attributed to many factors. This species was once native to the Midwest and southern Canada but is now no longer present in some states and a rare sight in others. The consolidation of barns and other man-made structures that used to lend the skunk shelter and hunting grounds, as well as the general modernization of farming, are factors linked to the spotted skunk's decline. Additionally, pesticide use, over-trapping, and natural predation are all having a negative effect on skunk populations.

EUROPEAN OAK

QUERCUS ROBUR | LEAST CONCERN

The Celtic word for oak is "daur," the origin of the modern English word "door," and thus the concept of doorways to the Otherworld was bound into the very meaning of oak trees for the Ancient Celts. The Tree of Life, or "Crann Bethadh," is a tree in a graphic representation of harmony and balance, nature's power coming together in an intertwined lacework of beauty, symmetry, and resilience. Oak trees, with their impressive size, longevity, and strength, were worshiped and seen as sacred beacons for the gods. The Tree of Life embodies the interconnected nature of the world, with branches that reach up into the sky and roots that reach down into the earth, and both meet in the trunk, creating a circular symbol for life.

Currently, the European oak is a species of least concern, however it is included here because forests, which are full of native flora, are increasingly vulnerable due to pests, disease, and climate change. Weather stress is causing damage to the bark of this tree, which in turn leaves the trees susceptible to ravages of insects, fungi, and disease. Trees are central to ecosystems and habitats, and if these trees fall in the forest all the flora and fauna are affected.

FINNISH FOREST REINDEER

Rangifer tarandus fennicus | VULNERABLE

The Sámi people of Sápmi have an intricate relationship with reindeer. They are semi-nomadic reindeer herders, moving through the inhospitable environments and treeless tundras alongside the migratory reindeer. To the Sami, reindeer are closely tied to life itself. One ancient story tells of a constellation in the night sky, a hunter with a bow aimed at the cosmic reindeer in an eternal hunt. When the arrow finally strikes the reindeer, there will be an apocalypse or end to the world. The Sámi and other reindeer-herding indigenous people in the Siberian subarctic regions maintain a delicate balance and harmony in their relationship to the creatures.

For the Koryak people in Far Russia, reindeer are also respected, sacred, and an integrated part of their daily life and survival. The Koryak have a legend of how Raven, the creator and first-ancestor, flew out into the stars, and returned bringing reindeer to the people.

Reindeer, or caribou, as a species are considered vulnerable, as their numbers continue to dwindle due to climate change, shifting vegetation patterns, and ineffective land use. Some sub-species of reindeer have already gone extinct, while others remain rare and threatened, like the Finnish forest reindeer.

FOUR-BLOTCHED UMBRELLA OCTOPUS

CIRROCTOPUS HOCHBERGI | ENDANGERED

The chief of the Ngati-Kahu-Nguna tribe told a story to New Zealand historian and ethnologist T. W. Downes, recorded in 1914. The chief spoke of the history of the white dolphin (Grampus griseus) known to the Māori as Tuhi-rangi, or, as the white New Zealanders named him, Pelorus Jack. Tuhi-rangi would swim alongside ships, escorting them through a dangerous channel in Cook Straight.

The chief tells the story of Kupe, who found some new islands "at the far end of the sea." This discovery came about because Te wheke-a-Muratangi ("wheke" in Māori means octopus) kept stealing all the bait from Kupe's fishing lines. Despite the advice of priests to tie his lures tighter, the clever and troublesome Te wheke-a-Muratangi still managed to steal his bait, afterwards fleeing to a safe distance.

Kupe sought the advice of priests, who told him that he was to follow Te wheke-a-Muratangi. Tuhi-rangi/Pelorous Jack would be his guide to keep him safe from danger. He was only to hunt the wheke through waters where his dolphin guide indicated.

Following these instructions and carefully trailing Tuhu-rangi, Kupe took his wife and family on his canoe. At last, he was able to track down Te wheke-a-Muratangi in a cave in New Zealand, whereupon a battle ensued, and Kupe emerged victorious. Afterwards, Kupe continued along the island and through the harbours, naming them as he went. Tuhi-rangi took up his post near French Pass, where he has guided and protected ships from dangerous rocks, eddies, and whirlpools ever since.

Octopuses in and around New Zealand are threatened by overfishing, and specifically the trawling fishing method. The loss of coral reefs as habitat due to climate change is also a factor in their dwindling populations. These creatures have a long lifespan but slow growth, which makes it difficult for them to adapt and recover from hardships.

GOLDEN-CAPPED FRUIT BAT

Acerodon jubatus | ENDANGERED

One of the most feared mythic creatures of Filipino lore is the Aswang. The Aswang masquerades in the daylight as a beautiful maiden, but the reality is a vampiric witch who shape-shifts at night into a bat. She glides under the moon and stars, and with her long proboscis reaches through the roof of the house of her victim and consumes their heart and entrails. Because an Aswang looks like any other human in the light of day, the way to discern their true identity is to gaze into their eyes, and if your reflection is upside down then they are a supernatural being.

Ironically, the fearsome stories inspired by the impressive size and wingspan of fruit bats, otherwise known as flying foxes, are unsupported by the reality of their gentle fruit-eating diet, and their vulnerability with having their roosting places disturbed. There are some fishermen who do not fear flying foxes, and instead when they find the creatures roosting in the tangled mangroves above their fishing grounds, see them as an omen of a prosperous excursion.

As the largest bats in the world, golden-capped fruit bats inspire both fear and respect. As pollinators, they are a vital cog in the machinery of the rainforest ecosystem, dispersing the seeds of the fruit from which they feed. These creatures are considered endangered due to deforestation and poaching for bushmeat.

GOLDEN SNUB-NOSED MONKEY

RHINOPITHECUS ROXELLANA
ENDANGERED

The travels and adventures of the Monkey King, Sun Wukong, are best known from the sixteenth century book, *Journey to the West*.

Sun Wukong is a trickster god. He was born whole, springing from a rock. At first, he went to live among the monkeys of the forest, and quickly attained status as their king when he proved his bravery by jumping from the great height of a waterfall. He led the monkeys in exploits and mischief. In his adventures he acquired, through cleverness, chain mail armour, cloud-walking boots, and a magical eight-ton staff.

His pranks and stubbornness escalated with his fame. Eventually, he decided to challenge the Jade Emperor. This infuriated the Jade Emperor, and Sun Wukong was imprisoned under a mountain to reflect upon his misdeeds.

After 500 years, he was finally freed by a Buddhist monk, and he became the monk's body-guard. Over the course of their westward journey, he underwent a spiritual transformation from an empty and ignorant monkey to an enlightened king.

Golden snub-nosed monkeys are heavily impacted by changes in their diet and habitat, and so deforestation is the largest danger to their population. Additionally, lichen is a main food source for the golden snub-nosed monkey, but lichen grows on fallen trees, which are heavily harvested, reducing the quality of food and habitat of this creature. However, they share a habitat with giant pandas, and so it is possible they will benefit from much of the conservation efforts that are put forth for pandas.

HAINAN MAGPIE

UROCISSA WHITEHEADI
ENDANGERED

The Chinese Qixi Festival happens on the seventh day of the seventh lunar month, and the story told on that day is of the romance between the Cowherd and the Weavergirl. This tale originates in the Han Dynasty, with the earliest reference in Shijing, known as Book of Odes. This book is the oldest collection of Chinese poetry. In the original text, there was no romance, but instead simply a mention of the Heavenly River, with the stars Altair, Vega, and Aquila as Herderboy, Weavergirl, and the Magpies. The lovers' tale evolved in the centuries following.

Weavergirl was a celestial being, and the youngest of seven sisters. She and the Cowherd, who was human, fell in love, and so she went to live with him upon the Earth. Her marital bliss, however, led to her neglecting her heavenly duties and earning the ire of the Jade Emperor.

The lovers were separated in the heavens. The Milky Way spills in a glistening, heavenly river, and forever keeps the lovers apart, except for once a year, on the seventh day of the seventh lunar month, when all the magpies of the world fly up and form a bridge of wings. On this day, the Cowherd and Weavergirl might briefly touch, before spinning back to their corners of the sky. This is one of the reasons why magpies are considered auspicious birds and bringers of good fortune.

There are some limited conservation efforts for this magpie species, however the auspicious Hainan magpie, also known as the white-winged magpie, is a rare creature with a low population that is endangered due to habitat loss and hunting.

HISPID HARE

Caprolagus hispidus | ENDANGERED

In Buddhism, Shakyamuni Buddha was a paragon of selflessness throughout his many incarnations. In his sixth life, he was reborn as a rabbit. As a rabbit, he was possessed of great virtue and goodness, and he gained as friends and followers other forest creatures. The rabbit lived well and taught the other animals how to behave with generosity and kindness. The god Indra heard of the rabbit, and disguised himself as an old man, coming to visit upon a holy day when the rabbit had taught all the animals that they must offer alms to anyone who passed through the forest.

The old man tottered through the woods and begged for food, and presently a monkey appeared and gifted him with nuts from the trees. A fox bore a fish he had caught and presented it to the hungry elder. But the rabbit had not found anything with which he could gift and feed the man, for the dried grasses he himself ate would not suit the man.

At last, empty-pawed, the rabbit hopped forth, and as the old man sat before a fire to warm himself, the rabbit hurled his own body into the flames as a sacrifice to the unknown stranger. Indra was so stricken by the unexpected offering, he gathered the dead rabbit in his arms and laid him to rest in a palace on the moon, so that today when one gazes up to the sky, the rabbit can be seen there in the shadows on the moon's face.

Agriculture, flood control, and human development have fragmented the habitat of the hispid hare in the foothills of the Himalayas in Nepal, Bangladesh, and India. Additional threats arise from natural predation and human hunting, but also from controlled burning for both agriculture and conservation of other local species, such as the tiger.

KIRIKUCHI CHAR

SALVELINUS JAPONICUS | ENDANGERED

There are many ghosts, restless dead, in Japanese folklore. One type are the funayūrei, or "boat spirits." These are the ghosts of those who perished upon the waves, in shipwrecks or near water. They have attributes of the sea and appear as humanoids with fishlike scales. It is said they seek to drown more humans by filling boats and making them sink.

In legends, sometimes the ghosts appear floating over the water's surface, or there are entire ghost ships manned by funayūrei, or they are simply eerie ghost lights. A shimmer and flash of sunlight glints from the spotted scales of a fish — or is it a hungry funayūrei lurking under the dark surface of the water?

Human disturbances to the habitat of the white spotted char are a threat to these fish, as are degradation of their freshwater habitat and overharvesting. Additionally, this species is undergoing a loss of genetic diversity as hybrid fish are released in their waters. This means that native char in the wild are fewer and fewer as hybrid fish outcompete for territory and mates.

Pronunciation: Kear-y-koo-chee

LONG-SNOUTED SEAHORSE

HIPPOCAMPUS GUTTULATUS
DATA DEFICIENT

From the Ancient Phoenician city-state of Tyre, one of the earliest depictions of a hippocampus can be found showing the god Melqart riding upon a creature that has the head of a horse, tail of a dolphin, and wings.

The name that we know this beast by, the hippocampus, comes from later Greek mythology. Poseidon, god of the sea, rode in a chariot drawn by these mythic creatures who had serpentine coils, fish-fin manes, and horse heads. They cut through the waves of the sea with the swiftness of equine mounts upon land and with the fierce wildness of the tumbling ocean waves. When fishermen caught seahorses in their nets, they were said to be the offspring of Poseidon's hippocampi.

The long-snouted seahorse is a rare creature, and so there is not enough data to form a conservation status. However, due to warming oceans and over-pollution, the illegal pet trade, and Chinese medicine, all seahorse populations are in decline.

LONG-WHISKERED OWLET

Xenoglaux loweryi | VULNERABLE

Birds were an important part of the culture of many Andean societies. Feathers were used for beautiful adornment, and birds' likenesses were carved on friezes, ceramics, jewelry, and weapons. These would have been sacred and cherished artifacts, as it was believed these likenesses carried with them the mythological, and therefore godlike, traits of the birds.

The Moche, a pre-Incan society in Peru, believed owls carried fallen warriors from the battlefield to the world of the dead. The owls bore their charges away in their claws, sweeping with their silent wings beyond the reach of the mortal cloud forests of the Andean mountains.

The cloud forests of the Andean mountains are the only known home to the long-whiskered owlet, a rare creature. It is endangered due to the deforestation of its limited habitat range.

LUSCHAN'S SALAMANDER

Lyciasalamandra luschani | ENDANGERED

The vision of the ferocious and deadly scaled, winged, and fire-breathing dragon came about in the Middle Ages. Dragons were mentioned in Ancient Greek mythology, and their relatives are serpentine mythical creatures from Asia, but during the Dark Ages when there was little literacy, and stories were only passed by word of mouth, the tales became woven together into chimerical beings. There is a bit of the salamander threaded into the dragon mythology as well, for salamanders were long associated with fire. Ancient Greek philosophers Aristotle and Pliny claimed that salamanders had the ability to resist and even completely extinguish fire, engaging with flames as a warrior might engage an enemy.

Perhaps because of their habit of choosing dry wood to nest in, when logs were placed in the hearth and set ablaze, the salamanders would scurry forth. The cause and reaction were conflated, leading to a belief that salamanders were the cause of the fire, or spirits of ember and flame.

The Luschan's salamander is an endangered species that is mainly threatened by its naturally restricted range, making it susceptible to ecological disasters and climate change. It is also in danger due to forest fires and over-collection by humans for scientific and trophy purposes.

MALLEE EMU-WREN

Stipiturus malachurus | ENDANGERED

The oozlum bird is a creature of Australian and British folktales. It is a quirky being, large enough for a man to ride upon, and it is incredibly vain. Instead of normal flight, it flies backwards in order to admire its own beautiful tail feathers. A side benefit of flying backwards is that it can see where it has been with much more clarity, though it doesn't know where it is going. If startled, it takes off, spiralling in circles, until it disappears completely.

Comparing oneself or another to the oozlum bird is often meant as mocking criticism of one's arguments as useless or inane. In other words, nonsense.

The mallee emu-wren is endangered due to habitat loss. It requires open mallee woodland with spinifex grassland. The grasslands are particularly vulnerable due to too-frequent wildfires and excessive controlled burning. This results in significant fragmentation and an inability of conservation efforts to regulate and preserve.

MARGAY CAT

LEOPARDUS WIEDII | NEAR-THREATENED

Among the folktales and legends of oral tradition that were collected by the American folklorist Elsie Eusebia Spicer Eells in the early twentieth century, was the tale of Domingo's Cat from Brazil.

Domingo was a very poor man, and at one point his circumstances were so reduced that he had to sell all his belongings and had no home or food; but he could not bear to part with his beloved cat.

The cat, in gratitude and devotion, ran off into the jungle and dug through the dirt, and in the flying debris there were pieces of silver that glittered in the light. He gathered up the silver and brought it home to his master. He then gathered some extra silver and brought it to the king. When asked where it came from, he told the king it was a gift from his master, Domingo. Over the next few days, the cat dug up gold, and then diamonds, and each time brought to the king as a gift from Domingo. The king decided Domingo must be very generous and rich indeed and decided his daughter must marry him.

The cat acquired a precious wedding suit, and defeated a giant by transforming him into a mouse and eating him, thus gaining a castle estate for Domingo, who married the king's daughter and lived happily. And then the cat wandered off into the jungle to find some other soul to benefit.

The margay was widely hunted until the late 1990s, greatly decreasing its population before conservation efforts began. Today, the cat's population is still in decline due to loss of habitat from deforestation in central South America.

MIGRATORY MONARCH

DANAUS PLEXIPPUS PLEXIPPUS
VULNERABLE

The Mazahua people of Mexico called monarchs "daughters of the sun" for the brilliant colour of their wings, and because the arrival of the monarch migration meant the arrival of the spring sun. They were revered and used as living tribute; they were also used in jewelry and adornments.

Several indigenous legends say monarch butterflies are the souls of children who have died; and they are welcomed back to the boughs of the trees in Mexico on the Day of the Dead.

The Aztec death goddess Itzpapalotl, meaning "Obsidian Butterfly," was both a patron to and a warrior who ruled over Tamoanchan, the land of birth and death, where women and children who did not survive childbirth would go.

There are two migration populations of monarch butterflies: eastern and western. As of 2022, the western population was counted at less than 2000 individuals. The eastern population is larger but is also in decline, as most of the milkweed habitat is gone. To help counter this, conservation efforts emphasize the importance of residential gardeners using native plants, particularly species that monarchs require for nectar. These efforts also emphasize using milkweed, which the monarch requires for its larval stage.

MOJAVE DESERT TORTOISE

GOPHERUS AGASSIZII | CRITICALLY ENDANGERED

The creator, called Mastamho by the Mojave people, was descended from the Earth and the Sky. He made people, crafting a son and daughter from his own body, from whom all other people were born. Along the banks of the Colorado River, he made a home for his children, giving them crops to grow corn, tobacco, and mesquite; and he taught them how to plant and tend them.

When Mastamho created other living beings, they were alike and very similar to humans in appearance. He didn't know what each might specialize in. He had them compete by running, jumping, and swimming. As they did so, he determined which would run on legs, which would fly, and which would swim, and then he went among them all and gave them names: birds, dogs, fish, reptiles.

In Mojave culture, the land and its creatures are revered. The desert tortoise is a creature native to the Mojave peoples' land and is a significant creature that features heavily in the song and storyscapes that the Mojave tell of their origin, history, travel routes, and celestial events.

The stories tell of Spirit Mountain, from which people first came, and to which they will return upon death. The physical mountain itself is Avi Kwa Ame National Monument. The mountain and its surrounding areas are sacred to the Mojave as well as a dozen other tribes, and it is home to the desert tortoise.

Tortoises are made to survive difficult terrain and high temperatures, but they cannot cope with the various dangers that humans pose, from land-use development to off-road vehicles, mining operations, solar farm expansion, and even diseases introduced by pet tortoises released into the wild. Humans present many threats to these creatures. The desert tortoise is a long-lived, low-reproductive species, and therefore rapid human development and expansion are outpacing them and have a significant negative impact on their survival and growth.

ORNATE EAGLE RAY

AETOMYLAEUS VESPERTILIO | ENDANGERED

The Māori knew stingrays as symbols of wisdom and protection, for they glide through the waters with grace and serenity. Yet when they are threatened, they can use the spines of their tails to great and deadly effect. They move swiftly, while camouflaging with the ocean floor, and they are not to be underestimated. Some communities of Māori still believe in ancestrally linked guardian spirits, and among those spoken of are shark, stingray, and owl. These guardian spirits are deities that have joined with an animal. The animal-deity's role is to guide and protect their descendants, but also to punish them if they stray to villainy.

Kaitiaki is a person or conservator over some precious piece of the natural world, like a river. The concept weaves disparate elements of ancestral beliefs, community, and environmental stewardship together into modern practical purposes. Stingrays are seen to be Kaitiaki of certain shores and beaches, to ensure shellfish are harvested in a way that does not hurt the web of the ecosystem, thus ensuring there are always plenty of shellfish and other resources when needed.

Ornate eagle rays have relatively long lives with few offspring and cannot recover easily when populations are impacted. These rays, and others, are often victims of overfishing in their habitats, which, as yet, have no protective conservation efforts in place.

PACIFIC POCKET MOUSE

PEROGNATHUS LONGIMEMBRIS PACIFICUS
ENDANGERED

The Miwok tell a tale of the "Stealing of Fire." Lizard was the first to catch sight of fire in the valley below, and he took the news to the others and to Coyote. Finally, it was decided that Mouse, the flute-player, would be sent to take some fire from that distant assembly house. Mouse set out, taking four flutes with him.

As he descended into the valley assembly house, he played sweet music with his flute. The sound drifted through the air and lulled the people to sleep. When all was still, he crept into their village and to the fire, placing the stolen bit into his flutes. The ember burned steadily in that safe cache, bright in the darkness of night. He swiftly made his escape.

The people woke and gave chase. Eagle, Bear, Rattlesnake, and Mountain Lion pursued, but the mouse managed to elude them, arriving safely with his flutes filled with fire. He deposited the contents of the flutes down through the cold smoke hole of the assembly house, playing his flutes as he did so to distribute the fire among the people. Because of an unequal distribution of the fire, the people of the vast assembly house were given different languages, ways of speaking, and customs of cooking and preparing their food.

The Pacific pocket mouse was thought to be extinct until 1993 when it was discovered and immediately classified as endangered. These creatures live along the coast of California, and only inhabiting such a specific and small region makes them susceptible to any habitat changes and impacts, such as road construction and global warming.

PHILIPPINE EAGLE-OWL

Bubo philippensis | VULNERABLE

In the pantheon of the Visayan people of the Philippines is the omniscient diwata Dalikmata. The goddess is depicted as a beautiful woman with thousands of eyes on her body, each of which is gifted with clairvoyance. She sees the past, present, and future, and she sees each person and knows all actions. At night she weeps for the ill actions that she sees humans doing to one another. It is said the dewdrops on the plants in the morning are the tears she has shed, and these tears can be a powerful ingredient for medicines.

As an intermediary between the human and spirit worlds, she takes her charge of watching over human souls seriously, and so she puts eyes on the wings of a butterfly to remind humans of goodness during the day, and she sets the eagle-owl to watch over the night.

The Philippine eagle-owl is experiencing rapid population decline due to deforestation and hunting. It is also vulnerable to natural forces that affect its habitat, such as typhoons and invasive pest species. Forest conservation is, as yet, not in place, but it would be an important first step to maintain the owl's habitat as well as the habitat of the rodents and amphibians it feeds on.

RED WOLF

Canis rufus
CRITICALLY ENDANGERED

The Pawnee Nation flag and seal features a profile of a wolf at the center. The wolf embodies the courage and cunning of the Pawnee. They were referred to by other Plains tribes as the Wolf People, out of respect for their tenacity, strength, and war prowess. When hunting, they strove to have the sense and stealth of the wolf.

The Milky Way is called the Wolf Road. Due to Earth's orbit, Sirius, the Wolf Star, passes the sun and disappears for part of the year. It appears in the evening in winter and in the pre-dawn hours in summer. This appearance and disappearance of the Wolf Star was said to be the coming and going of the wolf from the spirit world, running back and forth along the trail of the Wolf Road.

The red wolf is critically endangered due to poaching, trapping, and habitat loss. It is the world's most endangered canid. They are important to the balance of their ecosystem because as an apex predator, they play a vital role in maintaining the populations of deer and smaller mammals. The red wolf is an "umbrella species," which means that if their population is healthy, then so too is the overall health and balance of the entire region.

RESPLENDENT QUETZAL

Pharomachrus mocinno | NEAR-THREATENED

The resplendent quetzal, with its beautiful shimmering train of metallic blue-green feathers, was sacred, precious, and divine to many Mesoamerican civilizations. The Ancient Aztec deity, Quetzalcoatl, the Feathered Serpent, was inspired by the quetzal. Quetzalcoatl's serpentine body is adorned with iridescent green feathers, and the snaking, long body is like the quetzal's whipping train of feathers when in flight. Quetzalcoatl was a god of vegetation, earth, and water, and could also control the winds.

In Guatemala, the quetzal is a symbol of freedom, because its nature does not allow for it to survive captivity. If captured and kept in a cage, the bird will spurn food and water and die rather than live as a prisoner.

The resplendent quetzal is near-threatened, and its population is decreasing due to trophy hunting and trapping for the exotic pet market. As they are unable to survive in captivity, becoming a pet is death to a quetzal.

Pronunciation: Kuht-saal

RIVERINE RABBIT

BUNOLAGUS MONTICULARIS
CRITICALLY ENDANGERED

The Khoisan of Africa have a tale about the origin of death. The Moon wanted men to know that the cycle of waxing and waning was equivalent to birth and death, and as she would wax she was born again — and so it was with humans too. She sent Hare with this message.

Hare deliberately perverted the message, leaving out the rebirth part, saying, "As I die and perish, so shall you perish." When Moon learned of this, she beat the wayward messenger with a stick, thus giving Hare a cleft lip, while Hare kicked out at Moon, and so the great gouges from his claws are the dark streaks and spots we see on the moon's surface.

There are many variations of this tale. In one version, Moon saw Hare weeping for the death of his mother. To comfort him, she gave him a message of the renewal of life. When Hare contradicted her, Moon struck Hare and confirmed the permanence of death. In other versions, it was not a deliberate change to the message on Hare's part; instead, due to forgetfulness, he stumbled in haste, fell upon his face, and split his lip, which is why the hare's lip is cleft.

The female riverine rabbit only produces one offspring each year, and so they are very slow to grow in population. In addition, their habitat is disparate and often used for agriculture and livestock land, causing destruction to the unique landscape that the riverine rabbit needs.

ROWAN

Sorbus aucuparia | LEAST CONCERN

Sorbus aucuparia goes by many common names, among them rowan, mountain ash, quickbeam, and witch hazel. The wood of the rowan was ascribed magical powers in many European folk beliefs. A forked stick from a rowan was used as a dowsing rod or wand, waved over water or a path, to influence deities and spirits. In Scandinavia, the devil was said to carry a forked caduceus of witch hazel.

In Wales, the tree was sacred in ancient times, called "pren cerdinen." It was believed the best way to deter witches and spells was with a bit of its wood. Witches would not come near any who were protected by it. People would carry twigs of mountain ash in their pockets when roaming at night or going on a journey. The wood was embedded into walls and around the frames of windows and doors so that no ill would ever come to the residents of the house.

It is thought that the nineteenth century name "rowan" comes from old Norse "runa," a charm, due to the beliefs in its ability to ward off evil and misfortune.

Over half of Europe's endemic trees are threatened with extinction, as they are under increasing attack from invasive pests and pathogens. This is of special concern because the forests are home to great biodiversity, and planted groves are subject to dieback (a condition where the tree begins to die from the tip of its leaves or roots), which hinders reforestation efforts.

SCOTTISH WILDCAT

FELIS SILVESTRIS
EXTINCT IN THE WILD

Among the thistles and heather of the Scottish Highlands, a lone traveller might glimpse a dark silhouette with a blaze of white fur upon the chest, stalking through the edges of the firelight. A sinuous tail weaving in the shadows would announce the presence of Cait Sidhe, a fairy feline.

Cait Sidhe is thought to be inspired by sightings of hybrid descendants of Scottish wildcats. It was believed that if a body was left unattended during a wake, Cait Sidhe might steal the soul of the deceased. To prevent this from occurring, those at the wake would offer entertainment to distract the frisky feline, playing music for it to dance, and posing riddles (because no fairy can resist such games).

The Scottish wildcat is extinct now because of hybridization with household domestic cats in the UK.

SEA OTTER

ENHYDRA LUTRIS | ENDANGERED

The Tlingit, an indigenous people of the Pacific Northwest, tell stories of Kushtaka, who are shape-shifting man-otters. When one comes across the Kushtaka, they often appear like any man, and through trickery, lure unwary souls astray. Their motivations are inscrutable. In some of the stories, they are malevolent, drawing poor Tlingit to their death in the cold sea or to be lost and alone to freeze. Other times they save a stranded man or woman by turning them into an otter to survive the harsh, frozen climate. In some stories, they play with a lone traveller's perceptions in a wily prank; in others they steal a woman away from her family for a time, so she becomes ensorcelled to be a wild creature living under the influence of the Kushtaka, running naked under the starlight, sleeping in the roots of trees, and eating raw salmon, only to be returned months later to her family otherwise unharmed.

Ranging throughout the Pacific, sea otters have been targeted by hunters for their fur for centuries. They are also vulnerable to oil spills, pollution, and in conflict with fisheries. Due to recent conservation efforts, their numbers have rebounded slightly from the extreme low of 1000 individuals in the early twentieth century, but they are still at low enough numbers to be considered endangered.

SEYCHELLES WOLF SNAKE

LYCOGNATHOPHIS SEYCHELLENSIS
ENDANGERED

Among the indigenous coastal peoples of Nigeria, Senegal, and in the African diaspora of South America, there is lore of Mami Wata water spirits. Mami Wata has the upper body of a human (most often female) and the lower body of a fish or serpent, and she is often depicted accompanied by a snake, which is a symbol of divination. The snake is coiled around her body and rests its head between her breasts.

There are stories describing Mami Wata entrancing her devotees when they are immersed in her waters, or boating, and she draws them into her watery spirit realm. There they reside in a paradise for a time, and upon their return to the human realm, they are blessed with spiritual and material growth and wealth. Mami Wata's nature is a duality of physical power, death, and destruction on the one hand, and spiritual reflection, life, and creation on the other.

This creature is endemic to the Seychelles' tropical and subtropical dry forests, and therefore they are very affected by habitat loss and at risk of any single event eliminating their entire population.

SLENDER-SNOUTED CROCODILE

MECISTOPS CATAPHRACTUS
CRITICALLY ENDANGERED

An African folktale describes the crocodile as a once-beautiful creature. He had glorious smooth, golden skin, and it was kept in this lovely state by his habit of diving into the muddy waters in the daytime, where he was protected from the harsh sunlight. He only came out of the water at night when the mild moonlight shone upon the world.

The other animals heard of Crocodile's lovely skin, for he was not shy. He wished to show off, and so he began to emerge from his murky haunts in the daytime to bask in the envious gaze of the other creatures. As their admiration grew, so too did his vanity. He wanted them to look upon him more and more, and so he came up from the murky waters more often, spending longer under the burning sunlight. His attitude became unpleasant as knowledge of his beauty inflated his ego. The other animals grew tired of his superiority and eventually abandoned him.

Each day that he lay in the sun seeking admiration made his skin uglier, coarser, bumpier, and darker, until it was a thick, scaled armour, and no one wished to look upon him any longer.

The slender-snouted crocodile was once widespread in both west and central Africa. They face habitat loss due to human expansion and agriculture, hunting for bushmeat, and poaching for their skins. Finally, because their main diet is fish, they are suffering from a lack of a sustainable food source due to overfishing.

SUN BEAR

HELARCTOS MALAYANUS | VULNERABLE

In Vietnamese mythology, the ruler of the divine pantheon was Ong Troi, "Old Man of the Sky." In later times, with the spread of Taoism, he became identified with the Jade Emperor. Ong Troi created the land and sea and sky, the rivers and the rain, the sun and the moon. Afterwards, he created animals. He crafted each form and face with the love of an artisan. Among his children were the goddesses of the sun and moon. When he was angry with the world, natural calamities occurred: floods, droughts, and storms.

His older daughter, the sun rooster, bears the sun across the sky. She brings light and life to the world. Her moon sister is the moon swan, and she bears the moon across the sky to bring light to the dark hours. The two were the providers of life and warmth to the earth each day. The two sisters share their marriage bed with the bear god. He is a lusty husband, and when a solar or lunar eclipse happens, it is said that the god is with one or the other of his wives.

The sun bears are vulnerable due to heavy deforestation and poaching. Sun bears are important to their ecosystems for a variety of reasons, but mostly because of what they eat: they feed on termites that threaten to fell trees; they eat fruits and disperse seeds, planting new trees as they graze; and they till the soil as they dig for insects.

TEMMINCK'S PANGOLIN

SMUTSIA TEMMINCKII | VULNERABLE

The reclusive and nocturnal pangolins are rarely seen, and this heightens the mythical shroud around their existence. Elders of the VaJindwi in Zimbabwe have been reminding people of the old myths and beliefs that lead people to see the beauty of and to instill a sense of reverence and respect for the pangolin in the face of poaching. The VaJindwi belief system and practices embrace mysticism and recognize evil spirits, as well as the benevolent spirits of animals and plants. To come across a pangolin is good luck, and the number of steps it takes indicates the number of good years that person will have. To injure or kill one is taboo.

Anthropologist Martin Walsh writes of Tanzanian Sangu belief that pangolins fell from the sky (uwulanga) to the earth, sent by Sangu ancestors, to bond to a human. The human and pangolin then undergo a series of rites of seclusion, singing, and dancing. If the pangolin sheds tears while dancing, it is an omen of good rains to come in the next year. Dry eyes mean drought. The savannahs and all the creatures that live upon them suffer if the rainfall is sparse. At the culmination of the Sangu ritual, the person and the pangolin were led into the bush by the elders, where a sheep was ritually sacrificed, and the pangolin buried — and in some accounts allowed to escape.

Of the nine pangolin species, all of them are protected and have IUCN statuses ranging from vulnerable to critically endangered. They are all at risk because of poaching for traditional medicine or ornamental trade. Global warming and human expansion factor in as well, as they cause habitat loss.

TIBETAN ANTELOPE

PANTHOLOPS HODGSONII
NEAR-THREATENED

In Ancient Greek mythology, Theophane was a beauty, a nymph, and the granddaughter of Helios, the sun god. Upon seeing her, Poseidon, god of the sea, was struck by her loveliness. He desired to have her for himself, and so he spirited her away to an island surrounded and protected by the cerulean swells of the ocean. Even there, her legendary beauty tempted suitors to come seek her out. To keep the men at bay, Poseidon transformed Theophane into a sheep, hiding her among his flocks, and took on the form of a ram for himself.

The offspring of Poseidon and Theophane in these forms was a winged ram with fleece of gold. The golden ram was later sacrificed to Poseidon, and its Golden Fleece became an icon of power and kingship.

The Ancient Greeks spun this tale around a creature of divine and distant origins. Possible inspirations for the winged and golden ram could have been the takin or Tibetan antelopes, who are even to this day sought out by poachers and killed for the golden fibers of their hides, and woven into luxury shawls.

In the 1980s, the Tibetan antelope, or chiru, were endangered, but because of protective laws against poaching they have recovered their population to the point where they are no longer endangered, but near-threatened. Even so, they are still poached to make scarves from their soft, warm underfur — it takes three to five hides to make one scarf.

TRI-SPINE HORSESHOE CRAB

Tachypleus tridentatus | ENDANGERED

As creatures evolved and died and sprang forth and the world churned and changed, the horseshoe crab remained unchanged. Now, after millions of years, they are considered "living fossils." Despite a span of over 400 million years, the four modern species are still nearly identical to their ancient counterparts.

In Japanese folklore, fallen warriors are said to be reincarnated as horseshoe crabs that eternally roam the seafloor and are celebrated in art. The horseshoe crab is called "kabutogani" in Japanese: warrior's helmet crab. A kabuto is a helmet that was worn by Ancient Japanese warriors and was part of the traditional armour worn by samurai. Horseshoe crabs were said to be the reincarnation of samurai warriors who fought at battles along the shores of Japan.

The tri-spine horseshoe crab are prehistoric creatures now endangered due to habitat loss — sea level rise and coastal erosion — and overharvesting for biomedical use. They are harvested because their blue-coloured blood is critical for testing of pharmaceuticals and medical devices. Their blood contains a unique substance that coagulates when contaminated by bacteria.

UMBRELLA THORN ACACIA

VACHELLIA TORTILIS | LEAST CONCERN

In Ancient Egyptian lore, the first gods were born under the thorny branches of the Tree of Life, the sacred acacia. The thorny trees were known as a tree of life and death. While the brewed leaves and the sweet flowers have many beneficial uses as healing herbs, as a natural defense to being over-grazed, acacias release a poisonous tannin in their leaves that can cause death.

Lusaaset was the Egyptian goddess of creation, the female counterpart to Atum, the male creator deity. The pair were worshiped in the city of Heliopolis as primordial beings, and acacias stood at the entrance to Lusaaset's sanctuary. In an early story of Osiris, god of the underworld, he was tricked and killed by his brother Typhon. Typhon put Osiris' body to rest in a large sarcophagus and sent it into the Nile. The waters washed the chest away, and it finally came to shore at the base of a large acacia. The tree's roots and branches grew around the sarcophagus, enveloping the box and its contents, and immortalizing Osiris within death.

The tree also has Biblical significance, for when God told Moses to build the Tabernacle, the instructions included the Ark of the Covenant made of acacia wood, and it is thought that Christ's crown of thorns was woven from acacia.

The acacia is currently a species of least concern; however, its population is diminishing. The notable diminution of any tree species is worrisome because trees are a resource for any regional flora and fauna, including humans. Paying attention to which tree species are struggling, and where, will help conservation efforts for whole ecosystems as well as various species within them.

Pronunciation: Uh-kay-shuh

VIRGINIA BIG-EARED BAT

Corynorhinus townsendii virginianus | ENDANGERED

In Iroquois lore, the pygmies are tribes of tiny people who live in rocky places, the Djogeon. They live in houses and dress just as other people, only they are small. When their singing or the rhythmic beat of their drums is heard, it is a sign to offer up gifts to the pygmies. The Djogeon gather up gifts, like tobacco, to use as "hunting medicine." The Djogeon people express gratitude by granting favours, good fortune, hunting charms, or a prosperous harvest.

There are many different tribes of Djogeon. One subset, the Gandayah, tend to the flora, protecting against disease and pests. If given offerings, they assist respectful Iroquois farmers, who then benefit from flourishing crops. Among the Iroquois, wild strawberries are symbols of life, thanksgiving, and blessing: ripened sweetness of springtime sunlight's kiss within a lush red fruit. The little people have a special affinity for the fruit. They guide the roots and vines along the ground and arrange the leaves to benefit the most from the life-giving sun. The Gandayah occasionally reveal themselves in various animal forms as an omen: a robin to indicate good news, an owl for warning, and a bat for a mortal struggle.

The big-eared bat is easily disturbed by spelunking humans entering its cave habitat. Global warming and deforestation play a role in this species' shrinking habitat and lead to population decline as well.

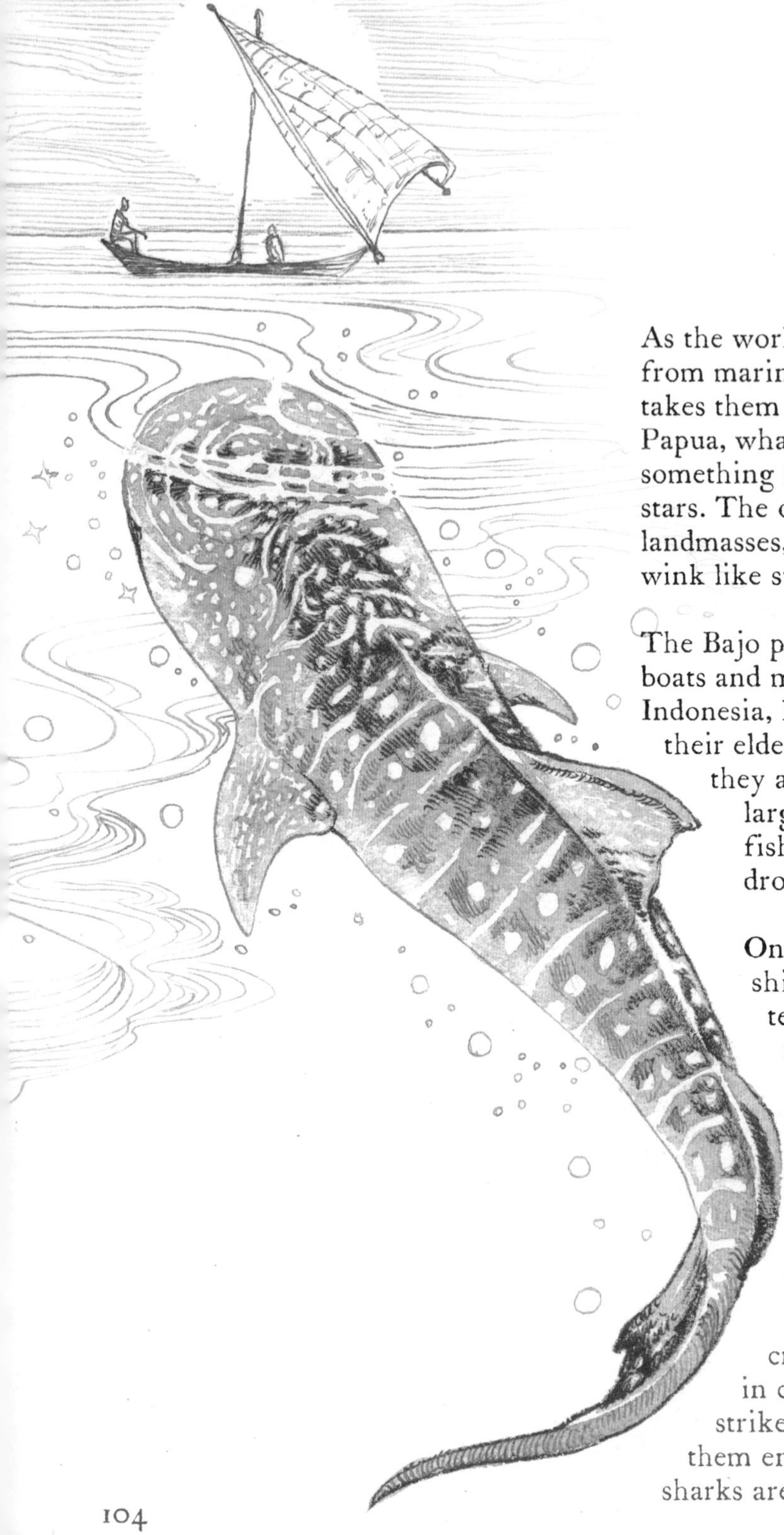

WHALE SHARK

Rhincodon typus | ENDANGERED

As the world's largest living fish, whale sharks have inspired awe from mariners over the millennia. Their long migratory path takes them through many island chains and coastal areas. In West Papua, whale sharks are called gurano bintang, "gurano" meaning something that comes from the east and "bintang" meaning stars. The open ocean is to the east of the nearby continents and landmasses, and the white markings on the creature shift and wink like stars seen through the water's rippling surface.

The Bajo people are migratory fishermen who live upon their boats and move through the waters and along the coasts of Indonesia, Malaysia, Brunei, and the Philippines. It is said by their elders that whale sharks are forbidden for hunting, as they are guarded by a spirit. Whale sharks, along with other large marine species guarded by spirits, are said to help fisherman in need, guiding them, or saving them from drowning.

One of the Swahili names for whale sharks is papa shilingi, which means "shark covered in coins." Kenyans tell of how the Creator looked upon the shifting surface of the seas, and sprinkled silver coins from the heavens into the water. The coins fell upon the whale shark, and thus the great creatures came to bear their striking coin-like markings across their backs and fins.

Whale sharks are long-lived and late-maturing creatures, which means they reproduce slowly. This, in combination with human threats like fisheries, vessel strikes, and global warming, has led the IUCN to consider them endangered. It is also known that hundreds of whale sharks are killed in China for their fins, skins, and oils.

WHITE-NAPED CRANE

GRUS VIPIO | VULNERABLE

In Chinese mythology, cranes are a symbol of longevity. They appear as design and art motifs. Their outstretched wings bear the deceased to heaven. They also transport immortals between the seams of the mortal and divine realms. One of the other Chinese symbols of longevity is the peach, which grows in the orchards of the goddess, the Queen Mother of the West. Together, cranes and peaches are often used in depictions of the Queen Mother's lush paradise isle. Etched in clay or sewn with shining silk threads into a tapestry, those symbols evoke the enchantment and divine aura of the immortal domain.

According to legend, cranes appear in four colours: white, yellow, blue, and black. A black crane is ancient, having already seen the passage of centuries. But a truly old black crane would further turn grey after it had aged another thousand years.

Due to habitat loss and overhunting, the white-naped crane is a vulnerable species. Ten of the fifteen crane species are currently threatened.

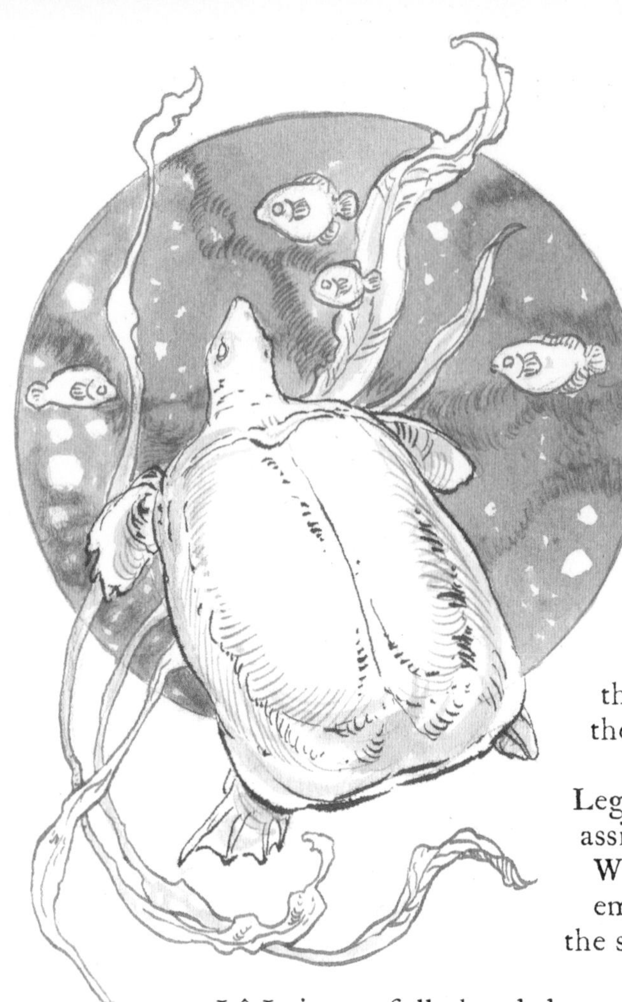

YANGTZE GIANT SOFTSHELL TURTLE

Rafetus swinhoei
CRITICALLY ENDANGERED

In the fifteenth century, Lê Lợi became emperor of Vietnam by rising against the Ming Dynasty and driving the Chinese peoples out of the country. Breaking the chains of that thousand-year rule was the beginning of the establishment of his own Lê Dynasty.

Legend says the deity, the Dragon King, provided Lê Lợi assistance in the form of a magical sword called Heavens' Will. Upon Lê Lợi's victory, the Dragon King sent an emissary, the Great Turtle God, called Kim Qui, to retrieve the sword.

Lê Lợi gratefully handed over the divine weapon to Kim Qui, and the spot where this exchange occurred became called "The Lake of the Returned Sword."

To this day, some of the last survivors of a critically diminishing population of soft-shell turtles inhabit that lake, and they are seen as the mortal incarnations of Kim Qui.

Once widespread in the fresh waters of China and Vietnam, loss of habitat and hunting have brought this species to where it is now: functionally extinct. As of 2023 there are only three known individuals alive and no breeding females. Despite these known facts, these creatures are elusive and difficult to detect, which means the great turtle god may yet resurface and confirm that the Yangtze giant softshell turtle may yet survive the anthropocene.

Pronunciation: Yang-see

WORKS REFERENCED

Australia Network News. (2014). "Hundreds of Sharks Killed Annually in Illegal Trade in China." ABC News. https://www.abc.net.au/news/2014-02-05/an-hundreds-of-sharks-killed-annually-in-illegal-trade-in-china/5239568

Bacon, J. R. (1900). The Voyage of the Argonauts. Small, Maynard & Company.

Bascom, W. (1981). "Moon Splits Hare's Lip (Nose): An African Myth in the United States." Research in African Literatures, 12(3), 338–349. http://www.jstor.org/stable/3818841

Bassette, K. (Waterspirit Clan), & Sharpback, R (Buffalo Clan). (1997). "How Skunks Came to Be." In D. L. Smith (Ed.), Folklore of the Winnebago Tribe, 93. University of Oklahoma Press.

Bastian, M. L. "Nwaanyi Mara Mma: Mami Wata, the More Than Beautiful Woman." Department of Anthropology, Franklin & Marshall College.

Barbeau, C. M. (1914). "Supernatural Beings of the Huron and Wyandot." American Anthropologist, 16(2), 288–313. http://www.jstor.org/stable/659612

Bassin, V., & Ender, K. (2009). "PAPA SHILLINGI Short whale shark documentary." East African Whale Shark Trust. https://vimeo.com/23125193

Beck, H. M. (2022). "Condor and Hummingbird." Inka World. https://inka-world.com/en/condor-and-hummingbird/

Bernier, H. (2009). "Birds of the Andes." The Metropolitan Museum of Art, Department of Arts of Africa, Oceania, and the Americas. https://www.metmuseum.org/toah/hd/bird/hd_bird.htm

Bettleheim, M. P. (2012). "Swinhoe's Softshell Turtle (Rafetus swinhoei): The Legendary Sword Lake Turtle of Hoan Kiem Lake." Bibliotheca Herpetologica. https://www.researchgate.net/publication/369143484_Swinhoe's_Softshell_Turtle_Rafetus_swinhoei_The_Legendary_Sword_Lake_Turtle_of_Hoan_Kiem_Lake

Beyer, H. (1908). "The Symbolic Meaning of the Dog in Ancient Mexico." American Anthropologist, 10(3), 419–422. http://www.jstor.org/stable/659861

Blaser, M. (2014). "Ontology and Indigeneity: On the Political Ontology of Heterogeneous Assemblages." Cultural Geographies, 21(1), 49–58. https://doi.org/10.1177/1474474012462534

Bleeker, C. J. (1973). Hathor and Thoth: Two Key Figures of the Ancient Egyptian Religion. Brill.

Dolitsky, A. B. (2002). "Ancient Tales of Kamchatka." Publication no. 19, Alaska-Siberia Research Center, Juneau, Alaska.

Diener, L. (1996). "Secret of the Crocodile and Other Animal Stories from Namibia," in Namibian Oral Tradition Project. New Namibia Books.

Downes, T. W. (1914). "Pelorus Jack. Tuhi-Rangi. " The Journal of the Polynesian Society 23, 3 (91), 176–180. http://www.jstor.org/stable/20701079

Eells, E. S. (1918). Tales of Giants from Brazil. Dodd, Mead and Company. https://www.gutenberg.org/cache/epub/21678/pg21678-images.html#cat

Emerick, C. (2014) "The Jogah: Little People of the Iroquois." Hubpages. https://discover.hubpages.com/education/Native-American-Fairies-and-Wee-Folk

Fenton, W. N. (1962). "This Island, the World on the Turtle's Back." The Journal of American Folklore, 75(298), 283–300. https://doi.org/10.2307/538365

Fletcher, A. C. (1903). "Pawnee Star Lore." The Journal of American Folklore, 16(60), 10–15. https://doi.org/10.2307/533670

Folkard, Richard. (1884). Plant Lore, Legends, and Lyrics Embracing the Myths, Traditions, Superstitions, and Folk-Lore of the Plant Kingdom. Sampson Low, Marston, Searle, and Rivington. https://www.gutenberg.org/ebooks/44638

Freidel, D. A. (1993). "Maya Cosmos: Three Thousand Years on the Shaman's Path." W. Morrow. https://archive.org/details/mayacosmosthreet0000frei/page/130/mode/2up

Gao, J. (2020). Saving the Nation through Culture: The Folklore Movement in Republican China. Contemporary Chinese Studies. University of British Columbia Press.

Gershwin, L. A. (2014). Stung! On Jellyfish Blooms and the Future of the Ocean. University of Chicago Press.

Gibbs, L. "Jakata: The Rabbit in the Moon". Mythology and Folklore UN-Textbook, University of Oklahoma. http://mythfolklore.blogspot.com/2013/06/jataka-rabbit-in-moon.html

Gifford, E. W. (1917). "Miwok Myths." American Archaeology and Ethnology, 12 (8), 283-338. https://digitalassets.lib.berkeley.edu/anthpubs/ucb/text/ucp012-010.pdf

"Itzpapalotl." Telleriano-Remensis Codex, folio 18 recto, MS Mexicain 385, Gallica digital collection. https://gallica.bnf.fr/ark:/12148/btv1b84582675/f62.item.zoom

The IUCN Red List of Threatened Species. Version 2022-2. https://www.iucnredlist.org.ISSN 2307-8235.

James, E.O. (1966). The Tree of Life: An Archaeological Study. BRILL.

Jochelson, W. (1904). "The Mythology of the Koryak." American Anthropologist 6 (4), 413–425. http://www.jstor.org/stable/659272

Johnsgard, P. A. "Cranes of the World: 8. Cranes in Myth and Legend." Papers in the Biological Sciences. University of Nebraska.

Joseph, K. (2023). "How Burning a Forest Can Help Gopher Frogs." Untamed Science. https://untamedscience.com/blog/how-burning-a-forest-can-help-gopher-frogs/

Kawharu, M. (2000). "Kaitiakitanga: A Maori Anthropological Perspective of the Maori Socio-environmental Ethic of Resource Management." The Journal of the Polynesian Society, 109(4). http://www.jstor.org/stable/20706951

Kenny, M. (1985). "Wild Strawberry." Wicazo Sa Review, 1(1), 40–44. https://doi.org/10.2307/1409425

Knightley, T. (1892)."The Fairy Mythology." George Bell & Sons. https://www.gutenberg.org/files/41006/41006-h/41006-h.htm

Koontz, R. (2018). "Landscape And Power in Ancient Mesoamerica." Taylor & Francis, 53.

Lawson, W. (1924). "Pelorus Jack: A Complete History of the Wonderful Pilot Fish of New Zealand." Pacific Marine Review: The National Magazine of Shipping, 459, 466.

Leeming, D. The Oxford Companion to World Mythology. Spain: Oxford University Press, USA. 394-395, 2005.

"'Living Fossil' Crabs Mysteriously Dying in Japan." (2016). Phys.org. https://phys.org/news/2016-09-fossil-crabs-mysteriously-dying-japan.html

Lopez, V., & Star Wolf, L. (2020). Shamanic Mysteries of Peru: The Heart Wisdom of the High Andes. Inner Traditions/Bear.

Pal, P. (1984). Tibetan Paintings: A Study of Tibetan Thankas, Eleventh to Nineteenth Centuries. Ravi Kumar, 132, fig. 61.

Pankenier, D. W. (2015). "Weaving Metaphors and Cosmo-political Thought in Early China." T'oung Pao, 101(1/3), 1–34, 2015. https://doi.org/10.1163/15685322-10113P01

Parker, A. C. (1912). "Certain Iroquois Tree Myths and Symbols." American Anthropologist, 14(4), 608–620. http://www.jstor.org/stable/659833

———. (1989). Seneca Myths and Folk Tales. Nebraska: University of Nebraska Press.

Pelton, M., & DiGennaro, J. (1992). Images of a People: Tlingit Myths and Legends. Bloomsbury Academic.

Perkins, D. (2013). Encyclopedia of China: History and Culture. Hoboken: Taylor and Francis.

Philippines, L. (2013). "Dalikamata." Visayan Mythologies. http://vizayanmyths.blogspot.com/2013/08/dalikamata.html

Pye, S. (2021). Saving Sun Bears: One man's quest to save a species. Signal 8 Press.

Ramos, M. (1969). "The Aswang Syncrasy in Philippine Folklore." Western Folklore 28 (4), 238–248. https://doi.org/10.2307/1499218

Ransome, H.M. (1937). The Sacred Bee. Houghton Mifflin.

"Resplendent Quetzal." (2023). American Bird Conservancy. https://abcbirds.org/bird/resplendent-quetzal/

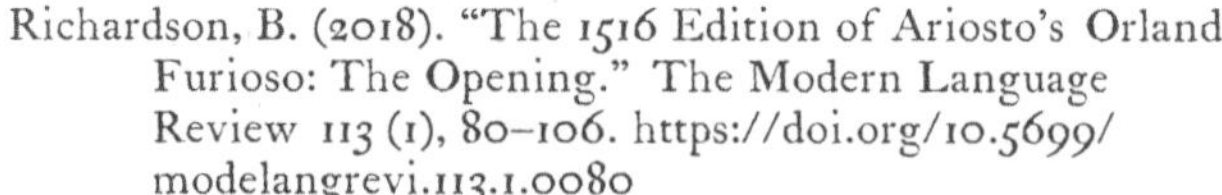

Richardson, B. (2018). "The 1516 Edition of Ariosto's Orlando Furioso: The Opening." The Modern Language Review 113 (1), 80–106. https://doi.org/10.5699/modelangrevi.113.1.0080

Richter, J. P. (Ed.). (1880). The Notebooks of Leonardo da Vinci, Book XX: Humorous Writings. Project Gutenberg.

Romera de Barajas, R. R. (1996). "The Maya Monkey." Mesoamerica Foundation. http://www.mesoamerica-foundation.org/https://blogs.uoregon.edu/mesoinstitute/about/curriculum-unit-development/stem/ethnozoology/monkeys/

Teit, J. A. (1921). "Tahltan Tales (Continued)." The Journal of American Folklore, 34 (134), 335–56. https://doi.org/10.2307/534923

The Angloinfo Mexico City Blog Team. (2017). "A Mayan Legend: The Resplendent Quetzal." https://www.angloinfo.com/blogs/mexico/mexico-city/mexico-city-is-my-home/1044-2/

Tindall, A., & Polidor, A. (2008). "Ward Valley." Sacred Land Film Project.

Tremain, C.G. (2016). "Birds of a Feather: Exploring the Acquisition of Resplendent Quetzal (Pharomachrus mocinno) Tail Coverts in Pre-Columbian Mesoamerica." Hum Ecol 44, 399–408. https://doi.org/10.1007/s10745-016-9827-8

Uddin, S. M. "Religion, Nature, and Life in the Sundarbans." Asian Ethnology, 78 (2), 289–310.

Urton, G. (Ed.). (1985). Animal Myths and Metaphors in South America. University of Utah Press.

Vicuña Cifuentes, J. (1910). "Mitos y Supersticiones Recogidos de la Tradición Oral." Impr. Universitaria, 23-24.

von fürer-Haimendorf, C. (1956). "Hans Abrahamsson: The Origin of Death: Studies in African Mythology. (Studia Ethnographica Upsaliensia, III.) Vii, 178 Pp., 17 Maps. Uppsala: Almqvist & Wiksells Boktryckeri AB., 1951. 60s." Bulletin of the School of Oriental and African Studies 18 (2), 394–94. https://doi.org/10.1017/S0041977X0010713X

Walker, J. (1966). Place of the Boss: Utshimassits. National Film Board of Canada. https://www.nfb.ca/film/place_of_the_boss_utshimassits/

Walsh, Martin T. (2023) "The Ritual Treatment of Temminick's Pangolin (Smutsia temminckii) among the Sangu of Southwest Tanzania", working paper. http://tinyurl.com/kxw4w3jb

Wassén, Henry. (1934)."The Frog in Indian Mythology and Imaginative World." Anthropos 29 (5/6), 613–658. http://www.jstor.org/stable/40446982

Werner, E.T.C. Myths and Legends of China. Dover, Reprint Edition, 1994.

"Weird Creatures with Nick Baker" (Television series). (2009). The Science Channel. Event occurs at 00:25.

IUCN RED LIST OF THREATENED SPECIES

In addition to the works listed above, this research has relied enormously on the extensive IUCN database, a comprehensive and up-to-date collection of sources and research on threatened species. This text used Version 2023-1, for the newest information, please visit: https://www.iucnredlist.org.

ABOUT THE AUTHOR

Stephanie Law's images trace the boundary between dream and reality. She delves into the pictorial language of allegory, explores mythology in new contexts, chases tiny worlds of wonder from an insect's viewpoint, and highlights the beauty of growth and decay found in nature. Growing up in California, Stephanie has been surrounded by the wealth of natural inspiration all around her. The twisting boughs of live oaks from the hills near her home insinuate themselves into her paintings. The chaos of Nature's wild growth, and conversely the beauty of decay, echo in the textures and fractal patterns of her work.

Early on, her career moved through the illustration and gaming world, but in recent decades she has focused more on her own body of work, gallery shows, and publications that promote environmental awareness and activism. Find her on the web at www.shadowscapes.com.

www.eyeofnewtpress.com